RED SKY

RED SKY

Matthew Petchinsky

1

Red Sky
By: Matthew Edward Petchinsky

Chapter One

It was a normal day like any other day, except the sky was the color of blood, red a deep red. The cause of this red sky is chemicals that our own government had released into the sky. They said the chemicals that the reluctantly released the names of the mixture of the exact chemicals they released in the sky to the public, were supposed to help fight global warming.

Unfortunately, they never told the other countries in the world at any United Nations meeting or letter. The result of the government not disclosing what they were planning to release in the atmosphere, caused panic in our neighboring countries that, they feared the atmosphere would deteriorate faster.

As a result of the fear of this, all countries of the world-built Spacecrafts to have their citizens to leave the planet to be safe.

That was about five years ago, my name is Greg, I am going to tell you a story of how things on earth are now. The news just came out saying that the chemical is striping away the atmosphere, slowly. We already lost 12% of the atmosphere in the last five years. I have been trying to find away to fix the atmosphere.

I was walking down to the local grocery store when I saw an old friend of mine, James, he is in his twenties close to his thirties, a little heavy set, he gained some weight since I last saw him, almond colored skin, Hispanic gentleman. He was working at the grocery store, when I approached, he saw me.

"Hello, Greg, how have you been?" James said.

"I am doing well, James. How have things been with you? I see you gained some weight." I said curiously.

"I am doing well. I am married now to my husband." James said.

I looked up at the sky.

"I hope your marriage has a future in this world." I said turning and walking into the store.

After thirty minutes of me being in the store, I stepped out of the store and went back home walking.

Most of the homes, I walked past had been long since abandoned and many have scorch marks from five years ago, when the sky turned red. Everyone panicked and rioted believing it was the apocalypse or rapture that "God was punishing mankind for it's sins" as mean believed.

Nearly 6 million died in those riots that night across the United States alone. After three days of rioting everyone calmed down and began to get to their rational minds and accept the sky as red.

Of course, many pointless deaths happened because of the irrationality of people. It is saddening to see people act like animals when something occurs like this. In fact, I know there have been riots even before the sky was red, like if a black out happened, just look at the entire history of irrational thoughts humans have.

Our government assured its own people that things would be okay and that it was the end of the world. As a result of other countries leaving except North Korea, all former lands that belonged to many other nations across the world, lay abandoned and unused, our government has sent expeditions to cultivate and take over the lands, wiping out any trace of the original inhabitants. Is our government great?

Chapter Two

When I arrived back to my home that was only five years old, still in great condition, it looked as if it was built yesterday. It was painted a beautiful silver color. I had chosen this color because it is beautiful, and I have never seen a silver color. I liked to be different from everyone else.

The front door was painted a blue color because, why not? Blue is wonderous and soothing.

I entered my home an unfortunately it wasn't very tidy because I hadn't cleaned in a while, there were stray papers from my research everywhere. My books were open on mythology and cryptoid zoology. The chemical not just turned the sky red, but it changed the electrical field of the earth and opened a portable where creatures entered into our world from their world. For the last five years, there have been reports across the country such as a whole flock of mothmen were flying in a group all over the state of Virginia and West Virginia to other cryptoid creatures roaming all over other states but in greater value, that people, everyday people caught them on footage. Last week a lady caught on her phone, a group of Wendigo entering a ski resort in the snowiest time of year in Colorado. About 30 or 40 people died from that attack.

Each year the sky is red, our worlds are blending as one. I have instruments that show that if the sky doesn't change back in a few years our ozone would be gone completely.

A sound of little feet ran across my kitchen floor. I grabbed a bat and went towards the kitchen. I switch the light on. There standing upright about two feet tall was a furry creature I had not seen before, this creature had thin arms, large ears, two fingers on each hand, two toes on each foot as well. The eyes were bright blue like sapphires. The creature growled at me, what the creature didn't know was that I rigged a trap in my kitchen, there was a cage was hanging just above the little creature. As it was distracted growling at me, it didn't notice that I flipped a switch on the wall that trigger the trap.

The trap fell fast and landed on top of the little creature. The little creature began to panic. I tried to calm it down, but it scratched my hand. The gashed were half an inch thick on my hand. I pulled out a cream that I had invented to heal myself quickly. I rubbed the cream on the gashes, and they were gone within 2 minutes painlessly. The cream I created took two years to develop, I didn't patent this because I don't want government hands on my formula.

How my cream works is it encourages new cell growth from the damaged cells. The cream has a small amount of uranium in it, since it has that, it gives it a green color to it.

I grabbed some thick rubber gloves from the kitchen counter, I grabbed the cage and took the little creature down to my basement lab.

I opened the basement door and turned-on light; the little creature had gone silent just glaring at me.

"Well, little fellow I am going to take you to your new home down in my lab, I can't wait to study you" I said to little creature as it gave me a frightened look on its face with its big blue eyes.

I walked down the stairs carrying the cage the little creature was in. when I got to the bottom of the stairs, I walked over to a laptop that was sitting on a worktable. I sat the cage with the creature inside it on the table. I turned on the laptop, when it finally booted up, a security camera program opened on the laptop showing a large room with around 30 or 40 different creatures, that I had captured in my home. Some of them were larger and deadlier than the little one, those were difficult to catch those took a tranquilizer to put them out.

I have been studying these creatures, they seem to have been giving off a radiation that doesn't seem to effect humans, it is like a background radiation.

I went to the phone to make a call to my girlfriend who is also trying to help me in my research, her name is Mindy. She and I have been researching these creature for the last five years ever since they began appearing on this earth.

"Hello, honey, could you come home quickly right after work? I have a new little friend I would like you to meet. I just caught him in our kitchen." I said.

"Yes, dear I will, it is a good thing we had the trap set in our kitchen.

Chapter Three

After the phone call, I went back to the kitchen to start preparing some food for my girlfriend and I. I left the little creature in the cage; I left the light on for it that way it doesn't get frightened in a new place.

I pulled out another laptop out that I kept in the kitchen and pulled up the security cameras that were in the lab. I had one pointed at our new little friend. I saw that he was pacing around the cage trying to figure a way out of the cage, he tried to gnaw at the bars, but they were too strong for him to gnaw through.

While I watched the live video feed, I began to get the grill ready in the kitchen for two 3-inch steaks from the grocery store. Very affordable at the price of $2.35 a steak that thick. Since the sky turned red and there wasn't that much of a population on the earth, especially in places where other countries just ruled. Our government started giving land up to farmers 100's to 1000's of acres of free land to anyone who wants it if a large portion of that land was for food production only.

For the last five years food supply has been more abundant than before which has cause the food prices to drop significantly.

In fact, I recall a time when before the sky turned red there was a pandemic ten years before the day of the sky turning red that caused food prices to rise because of inflation. As well, during that time of the pandemic fuel prices were outrageous as well, now that the sky is red, the fuel prices are at $0.50 a gallon. It is amazing what happens when the earth becomes basically empty from a large portion of humans.

I chopped up some onions and washed some small bell peppers, I poured two glasses of alkaline waters. I had two plates set on the table and utensils ready, along with two candles on the table as well.

Mindy came home a couple of minutes later.

"Hello, honey, I'm home." Mindy said as she walked in the door.

"Hi, honey, dinner is almost ready, just got to get a good crust on the steak and making sure it is medium rare." I said flipping the steaks.

"It smells delicious. I can't wait to eat, I'm starving." Mindy said.

Two minutes after Mindy got home, the steaks were ready, when I cut into the there was a beautiful crust on both steaks and right in the middle was a beautiful light pink with specks of red in the middle. It looked perfect. I sliced up both steaks, place three evergreen onions, two small bell peppers each plate. I set the plates on the table across from each other. Mindy and I each sat down at the table to eat.

"Well, honey, how was your day at work?" I asked while taking the first bite of my food.

"Work was good. Just been cataloging new creatures in the main containment facility, what is the count of the ones we have here?" Mindy said taking a bite of her food.

"I believe we have around 20 or 30 different creatures, have you been able to let your facility know about the creatures we have here?" I said taking a sip of my alkaline water.

"Yes, but they said the facility is over packed and can't take anymore in their facilities. They suggested that we terminate these creatures ourselves." Mindy said without hesitation in her voice.

"Termination of these miraculous creatures? I mean there are more that arrive each day, but I can't bring myself to destroy them." I said swallowing hard on my steak.

Outside the sky started to darken, but since the sky was red the clouds look dark red with rain and the rain itself looked like blood coming down from the sky. You get used to that after five years, but in the first few weeks after the sky turned red, everyone went on a riot believing it was the rapture again. They thought the world was going to end because people believed the sky was bleeding.

Mindy and I continued our meal, a loud thunder cracked above our house. I turned to look at the security feed. The creatures were all going crazy in their cages slamming into the walls and so was our new little creature we captured earlier today. Something about stormy weather caused these creatures to act violently.

"Looks like our specimens are going crazy again." I said turning back to Mindy.

"Yes, indeed. We must find away to get them away from the house, before they break out and harm us." Mindy said.

"I agree." I said.

After we ate of dinner, Mindy and I went down to the lab so she could take a closer look at the newly caught creature. When we entered the lab, the creature began to growl at the both of us.

"Someone is in a bad mood." I said as I approached the cage.

"He must be a smaller subspecies, much like a squirrel type of creature. Form what I've seen in the containment facility is that these little guys have a venomous bite." Mindy said pulling out a pair of gloves and a cotton swab for a saliva sample.

"Want me to grab him and hold him still so you can get your sample?" I asked.

"Yes, I will try to keep his eyes fixed on me." Mindy said.

I put on some think rubber gloves, opened the cage slowly, the creature started growling louder at me. I used one of my gloved hands to distract it as did Mindy as I used my other hand to reach around and grabbed him by the back of the neck like how you grab a cat. The little creature froze stiff as I lifted him out of the cage.

The little creature's mouth was gapped open. Mindy put the cotton swab in his mouth, she even took a sample of fur from the little creature. The little creature just watched with bulgy eyes helplessly.

"Okay, put him back in the cage, I got my samples." Mindy said taking the samples over to the testing equipment on the table opposite to the cage on the opposite table.

I put the creature back in the cage as quick as I could. After I let go the little creature scratched the rubber glove. Good thing the glove was a thick rubber because I didn't feel it.

Mindy put a small drop of the sample of the blood into a petri dish and into a scanner. The machine started to scan the sample, after a few minutes, about six or seven minutes, the machine printed off a breakdown of the DNA structure, radiation read outs, as well as possible diseases the little creature has.

The printout read that the little creature has a microorganism that isn't fatal to humans just other animal life, the radiation of the creature is a harmless radiation that is like background radiation. It is the radiation between worlds that is like a marker tag of that world. The DNA of the little creature is like a squirrel, mixed with cat, sloth, and kangaroo DNA mixed.

Chapter Four

Mindy was surprised at the data that came out from the machine. Suddenly the ground started to shake, the tables were shaking, and the little creature was freaking out. Mindy and I went to take shelter under the tables. The shaking intensified; car alarms went off outside. People were screaming.

Ten minutes later, the shaking stopped. Mindy and I crawled out from under the table.

"Go check the computer to see what the Richter scale says about that quake, I will go check our seismographs." I said heading to a small room in the back of the lab that we stored our seismographs.

The earthquakes have increased in frequency since the sky turned red and the arrival of these creatures across the globe, especially in places that never had earthquakes before.

Mindy and I have a theory that the portal or tear in our world's fabric or dimensional tear, whatever you wish to call it, is expanding and causing the earth to become unstable. Our instruments indicate that this earthquake was stronger than three days ago, in fact it was about 36% more stronger compared to three days ago.

Mindy and I tuned into the *CBS NEWS* channel on the TV, their studio was hit and they said that the state of California lost 15% of it's land from the quake. Turns out that roamer that California would lose some of it's land because of the earthquakes is true, but not how it was originally supposed to happen. There were other reports of Japan losing 58% of it's land, China lost 43%, Korea lost 63%, the Philippines were completely lost, Hawaii was completely lost, Alaska lost 34%, Russia lost 46%. The list could go on and on. Most of the world lost a lot od it's land, unfortunately if these quakes keep on their current path the whole earth could disappear from this dimension altogether.

Mindy and I looked at each other in shock for a moment, then back at the TV.

"This is the first time that any land began to disappear, how are we going to find away to fix everything?" Mindy said.

A government official came on to the TV to tell the nation that everything is okay like all government officials do in a time of crisis. How could lad disappearing be, okay? What are they hiding?

Mindy and I both knew that government officials were puppets, and they were reading a well-prepared script to try and bring peace of mind for the masses. Mindy and I turned off the TV and cleaned up the lab before heading back upstairs. Once we finished, we gave the little creature a bit of food and water before going upstairs. The little creature devoured the food within seconds and sipped the water like there was no tomorrow for him.

"Look, honey, he is eating and drinking fast." I said pointing at the cage.

"Awe, pour little guy." Mindy said as she turned to go up the stairs.

I followed Mindy up the stairs, when we got to the main floor of the house, Mindy went to the couch and fell onto the couch out of exhaustion. I went over to Mindy, lifted her legs, laid them over me as I sat on the couch and pulled off her shoes and began to massage her aching feet.

Mindy exhaled a long breath, she looked at me.

"The instrument read outs said that the atmosphere would be giving out in two years and if the quakes keep getting worse it maybe sooner then that." Mindy said.

"I am not sure how we could get the sky fixed. Although, I believe the answer may lay in one of the abandoned government labs ten miles from here." I said still rubbing Mindy's feet.

"We will go there tomorrow, first thing in the morning, they are not guarded so we won't get in any trouble." Mindy said turning on the couch to her right side.

The bases we are speaking of were responsible for research and development of the chemical that turned the sky red. Once the mission was accomplished the government abandoned these bases, even leveling classified documents behind. The bases were abandoned overnight, five years ago. The government got careless and left all classified documents behind, but no one dares enter these bases because they fear that that is where the creatures are nesting and originate from.

Chapter Five

The next morning, Mindy and I awoke early, before the sun arose, around 5:30am. I cooked us some eggs and packed us some Alkaline water, about two gallons each, some beef for lunch that was sealed in a 24hr thermal container that keeps the food warm and fresh all day.

Mindy packed the back packs with radiation protection suits, flashlights, knives, small portable shovels, pickaxe, and two Geiger counters. We want to be cautious because of the stories of toxic levels of radiation that are in parts of the abandon bases.

"Are things ready to go?" Mindy asked as she walked into the kitchen.

"Yes, they are, here is your coffee and eggs." I said handing Mindy a plate of eggs with a coffee that was a caramel coffee just how she likes it.

"I packed all the other essentials we need to explore the abandoned base." Mindy said taking a bite of her eggs and sipping her coffee.

I opened the laptop, I went to a map program and researched the closest abandoned base, it was ten miles away from our house to the west of us, another the was ten miles to the south of us and another ten miles to the east of us, and one to the north of us. Our plan was to try and hit all four of them.

The positions of the bases were very interestingly placed. It makes you wander if the government placed these bases in a position to isolate the people of this city.

There were rumors that the government was going to lock down our city fifteen years ago and run experiments on our inhabitants like mutation experiments on the inhabitants, but those rumors stopped once the government shut down the bases.

After we ate our breakfast, we started loading up the car. Within twenty minutes the car was loaded.

"Which one should we go to first?" Mindy asked starting the car.

"Let's start with the one to the north of us, these bases are all exactly ten miles from our house. There must be some reason for that. I find it quite convenient." I said taking a sip of water.

10 minutes later, we arrived outside the gate of the base. The gate was sealed with a chain, but it was corroded, and a bite rusted as well. I pulled out a pair of bolt cutters from the car, we had them in the car for any occasion. I cut the chain and the chain fell to the ground with the normal metal falling sound that was a bit satisfying, strangely enough. I pushed gate to the right, it was a bit difficult to move it because of the rust, Mindy brought over the *WD-40*. As I pushed the gate, she stood in front of me spraying the lubricant under the wheel of the gate making it move more smoothly.

Once we got the gate open, Mindy and I went back to the car. We drove passed the gate. I pulled up an old map of the base, the lab was located in the middle of the base. It was about three or four minutes away from the main gate that we entered in from.

Chapter Six

We arrived at a large building, that had overgrowth all over it. I pulled out the Geiger counter to check for radiation. The device showed no radiation in the area.

"It is all clear on radiation, we can step out here." I said, opening the car door.

Mindy stepped out of the car as well, we both grabbed out backpacks. I took the bolt cutters with us. We approached the front door of the building, the paint on the door was worn down, the chains that were holding the door had rusted away and fell to the ground with overgrowth on them.

I opened the door, the door creaked loudly, and gave a bit of a popping sound as well. When I got the door all the way open, Mindy was the first to walk in, inside was pitch black with blacked out windows. Mindy and I both pulled out our high-power efficient flashlights they ran for 12 hours on a charge and made the room that is pitch black be as clear as day.

The room we were in was a reception area, there was a small window to the left about six feet from the front door, where you signed in. I went to the window and saw a sign in sheet that was a bit molded, but still legible to read. It was dated five years ago, the day of the sky turning red.

When we got to the end of the room the was a turn that turns into a hall to the left, at the end of the hall, there was a double door that were glass, I say were because the glass had shattered and was all over the floor. I pulled out the Geiger counter out to test for radiation. Mindy looked at me concerned and a bit spooked because the atmosphere felt a bit off in there as if something was watching us.

"Is it clear of radiation?" Mindy asked with a concerned and frightened look on her face.

The machine beeped.

"Yes, all clear, the area is clear from radiation." I said walking forward down the hall.

Suddenly, we heard a crash come from behind the doors. I quickly pulled out a gun from my bag and Mindy pulled a gun as well. We each carried MP-5's for protection on expeditions such as this. These days since these creatures have been appearing we must keep well protected.

Mindy and I went through the double door, the crunching of glass below are shoes as we went through the doors. We saw scratches on the walls. The scratches were long and deep scratches. I gulped out of nervousness. Mindy was behind me.

We turned into a lab the was trashed and there were filing cabinets tipped over, there were ever computer monitors on the floor. Mindy went to on of the tipped over filing cabinets. I helped her lift it up off the ground. As she went through the files in the cabinets, I went to the computer monitor that was on the ground, I followed the connector cord to the main computer unit. When I saw the computer unit from following the cord. My hopes of salvaging something were lost when I saw that the computer unit was smashed to pieces and the motherboard was trashed as well.

Our only hope to finding any answer was the filing cabinets. I went over to another set of filing cabinets that were still standing, but full of overgrowth. I opened the first draw and I saw documents that indicated launch codes for rockets dated the exact date five years ago, on the day the sky turned red.

"Honey, I found the documents on the launch. The codes they used. I think this cabinet may have the formula they used to turn the sky red." I said excitedly.

Mindy came over to the cabinet I was at, when we heard a crashing sound from one of the other labs down the hall. I jumped and Mindy jumped from the loud noise.

"We might want to hurry and find what we need, I will go check it out, while you keep searching that cabinet." I said pulling out my gun and walking towards the hallway and turning to the right.

As I walked down the hall, I heard the crash again. I pulled my walkie talkie out of my pocket and told Mindy I was approaching one of the labs that I heard the crashing sound at. As I entered the lab, I heard a rustling sound coming from the other end of the lab. I shined my light in that direction, I saw a 8 foot tall Wendigo, it's face was a deer skull that had no skin on it, the was two brown eye balls staring at me, the antlers were 6 points. The Wendigo growled at me; I froze for a moment as I grabbed my walkie talkie.

"Honey, have you found what we need? We have a Wendigo here, staring right at me." I said over the walkie talkie.

"No, I haven't, get out of there, honey, run!" Mindy said with panic in her voice.

Chapter Seven

I turned as fast as I could and ran as fast as I could down the hall. The Wendigo pursued me, the beast roared as he pursued me. Mindy ran out of the Lab that she was in ahead of me. We were both being chased by the Wendigo. When we got outside, we ran to the car as fast as we could. While Mindy was trying to get the car started, the Wendigo burst through the doors, knocking the doors off their hinges.

As Mindy was trying to get the car started, the Wendigo jumped on top of the car, smashing the windshield. I got out of the car and was shooting at it, the Wendigo turned its attention to me. I took off running and the Wendigo chased me. Mindy manager to get the car started, she drove fast to catch up to me and picked me up within a minute, the Wendigo was chasing the car, the wendigo was roaring and growling at us as we tried to speed away for it.

When we got to the front gate, we hit the guard house crashing right through it, sending glass and other items flying. The Wendigo didn't give up its pursuit of us.

I got out of the car window and was shooting at him, the bullets bounced off the Wendigo, not leaving a scratch or slowing him down. I even tried to throw some small explosives at it, but it kept coming at us. Mindy hit the gas on the car speeding the car faster. We saw an opportunity to escape the Wendigo when we are turning right onto a bridge and the Wendigo couldn't keep up that it tumbled and gave a loud growl and roar from the tumble.

Mindy kept the car going fast, we got 12 miles away from where the Wendigo was, before Mindy slowed the car down. Our adrenaline was still high from the chase, I pulled the water gallons out and I opened it and took a sip and gave Mindy a sip of the water.

"That was quite a rush, did you find what we are looking for?" I said.

"No, we must check the other bases for what we need, but we need to get the car repaired first." Mindy said driving us home.

When we arrived home, it was already around 12pm. Mindy and I unloaded the car, after we unloaded the car, Mindy grabbed $6,000 from the saving for car repair. Everything may have gotten cheaper, but the damage the Wendigo caused was about $6,000 worth of damage to the car. Mindy left to go to the mechanic to get the car repaired, she even took an extra $200 that way she could go do some shopping and get some fast food as well.

I went down to the lab to try and get a computer extrapolation of the launch codes that we got. I was hoping it would give us more of an exact time slot at which these codes were used.

Chapter Eight

After two hours, Mindy returned home from dropping off the car to the mechanic and the shopping trip. Mindy got herself a *Whataburger* meal and got me *Popeyes* nuggets and tenders. I helped Mindy with the things she got from her shopping trip and the food. Mindy bought more ammunition for our weapons and some makeup, she is addicted to makeups, since they are cheaper now, she has and entire room of makeups.

I set the table so we can eat, I sat down and then Mindy sat down at the table, we both began to eat. Mindy took a sip of the tea that she got at the *Popeyes*; I drank ginger tea with my meal. I have been on a *kidney friendly diet* you could say because I have a history of kidney infections and kidney stones. I don't mind being on this diet if I am health. I know I am taking the medications we created, but I still after so many years of being on the *kidney friendly diet,* I have gotten used to eating the healthy meal and having fast food occasionally, if it is *Wendy's or Popeyes.*

"How long until car repairs are done?" I asked as I took a bite of my food.

"Three days, we will be back to exploring the abandoned bases in three days." Mindy said taking a bit of her meal.

Suddenly, the perimeter alarm went off. Mindy rush off the table to get the gun hidden behind the couch, I grabbed the gun hidden in the pantry. I went to the laptop and pulled up the outside security camera.

"Shit, we were followed." I said.

"What do you mean?" Mindy said confused.

"Our Wendigo friend followed us home and he brought four others with him." I said turning off all the lights.

I saw on the cameras that the Wendigos were peering into our windows, but they couldn't bust them down, they were a strong polymer, and our house doors were reinforced titanium steel. The Wendigos were banging on the walls, doors and windows trying to get in. They were circling the house. Mindy and I kept the guns loaded and were hidden away from sight.

The Wendigos were roaring and screeching outside of the house still circling. I typed on the keyboard and initialized a defense program that launched a tear gas and began firing at the Wendigo's heat signatures. These bullets however were enhanced with explosive capsules that exploded when it makes contact with the target. We heard roars and what sounded like screams from the Wendigos, after about ten minutes, the defense program stopped firing and the roars ended.

I took down the defense program, Mindy and I opened the back door and we saw all five of the Wendigos dead laying on our back porch. I grabbed some gloves and handed some to Mindy. We got on either side of the dead Wendigo and lifted the body.

We took each body to a large pit we had set up in the middle of our 12-acre land. We threw each body into the pit and poured lighter fluid into it.

When the bodies began to burn from us, putting a match and lighter fluid into it, the flames were large and beautiful, with colors of orange, red and blue. For some reason the Wendigo's body always gives the flames a blue tint. The bodies were completely charred after twenty minutes of burning.

After we finished burning the bodies, we sealed the pit with a metal lid, as well as a padlock. Mindy and I went to check out the damage on our home. We saw large claw marks, but not dents or broken windows.

"Good thing, our home is stronger than a fort." I said relieved that there wasn't much in the way of damage to the house.

"Yes, I am happy, but how did he track us? I could have sworn that he lost our trail." Mindy said with worry in her voice that other Wendigos might show up on our doorstep.

Chapter nine

After we cleaned up the bullet shells and finished our meal, we went to the bedroom to relax and watch a movie.

We chose to watch the 1990's movie *Tremors*. A very great classic movie.

I made us a big bowel of popcorn, along with some ginger tea. Mindy and I fell asleep from exhaustion that we missed the best parts of the movie.

Later that night, Mindy's fears came true. The perimeter alarm went off at 5 am in the morning. Mindy and I woke up to the sound of roars, explosions, and the perimeter alarm going off. I pulled up the security cameras, which showed forty more Wendigos around our property.

The defense system was shooting as many as it could and the secondary defenses were activated shooting other creatures that the first defense system missed.

After two hours of explosions and roars, everything got quiet. I did an infrared scan as well as a thermal scan. All the Wendigos were dead. Mindy and I got up to get ready for the day, but she had to be at work at 9:30 am. She quickly got ready and was out the door by 8:15am. I was left to clean up the deceased Wendigos.

I put gloves on and went to open the pit, now that pit was 60 feet deep, so it could fix all the forty Wendigos of course. I dragged each of the heavy Wendigo bodies to the pit. I could hear each one made a loud "thud" sound as they hit the bottom of the pit.

I was doing this task for five hours, after the five hours, I poured two gallons of gasoline into the pit and then tossed in a match. The flames burned beautifully, I sealed the pit, then went inside to take a shower. I drank four gallons of water doing that task.

Once I was out of the shower, Mindy called me.

"Honey, how are things going?" Mindy said.

"I am good, I took five hours to put the forty bodies down the pit." I said.

"Damn, that is a long time, I hope we don't get more of those Wendigos attacking us." Mindy said.

"I am not sure if they will attack again, just don't worry, have a good day at work, honey." I said trying to reassure her that things should be better.

"Well, I need to get back to work, I will see you tonight, I love you, bye honey." Mindy said hanging up the phone.

"I love you too, bye honey." I said also hanging up the phone.

I went down to the lab, when I arrived, the computer had finished its extrapolation of the launch codes. The computer printout said that the launch codes were used at exactly 5am, that way it would cause panic and scare people once the sky turn red.

"Wow, the Government wanted people and other countries to go crazy and cause chaos." Mindy said with shock in her voice.

I place the report from computer into a file that Mindy and I kept for our research we are doing on the whole red sky incident. I took a sip of the alkaline water that was by the desk.

Suddenly, the phone rang, Mindy went to get the phone. I was checking the satellites for any activity of the Wendigos near our home. So far, according to the reading there was a whole group of them 36 miles away from where we are located.

Mindy came back from getting the phone.

"Who called?" I asked still watching the satellite feeds.

"That was Jamie from down the road, she said that there is extensive damage around her property as if a group of large creatures were ripping up the trees and land. She wants us to investigate." Mindy said.

"Okay, I will get the equipment ready for our investigation." I said getting up from the seat in front of the computer.

I went to the supply room, I grabbed Geiger counters, cameras, measuring tape. I made sure the cameras had fresh batteries. Mindy grabbed backpacks with waters and snacks for us. Homemade jerky, much better than the ones that are made in the stores.

When I finished gathering the equipment, I pulled up in the front with our all-terrain vehicle that had a trunk as well sits two people. This one was a state-of-the-art vehicle that was able to carry over 12,000 pounds, onboard radar system, as well as harpoon with a tracker at the end. Mindy joined me five minutes later.

"I got the supplies loaded, let's get this investigation done with." I said opening the door for Mindy.

"Good thing it is a short distance from our home, the battery on this thing will last only 12 hours at a time." Mindy said.

"Well, we could upgrade it to solar energy soon." I said starting the vehicle.

After fifteen minutes of a drive down the road, Mindy and I arrived at our neighbor's home. Jamie was waiting for us, outside of her home. As I pulled in, Jamie waved at us. Mindy got out of the car first, then I did once I shut off the vehicle.

"Hey, Jamie. What seems to be the issue?" I asked.

"Hey, yeah. I found a lot of damage around the side of the yard there." Jamie said as she pointed us in the direction of the damage.

"Okay, we will get our equipment set up and begin our investigation." Mindy said turning towards the vehicle.

Mindy and I grabbed all the equipment we brought with us.

Upon first look at the damage, you could see several tall trees knocked over and stomped on by large feet except with three clawed toes. There were large footprints about 7 feet across. Mindy and I looked at each other with shock expressions on our faces.

"This is something new, I am picking up the same radiation as the other creatures." Mindy said.

"I need to cross reference the data with the earthquake data from earlier." I said getting ahead of Mindy finding a saliva sample.

Chapter Ten

I collected the salvia sample, when about 3 or 4 feet away from the saliva, was a large scale about a foot long, but had an iron ore color. I packed the scale up, I noticed the damage goes about 6 or 7 acres deep into the woods before ending.

"Honey, I am going to go get our vehicle, we need to go deeper. Did you bring the flares?" I said heading to the vehicle.

"Yes, they are in the glove box and center console." Mindy said following me to vehicle.

When Mindy and I got to the vehicle, I started the vehicle and started down the path of destruction. The onboard radar was beeping fast. Mindy looked at the radar and saw a larger signal being picked up by the radar.

"We have something coming at us from the west." Mindy said looking around.

I stopped the vehicle, and we were in the middle of the destroyed woods. I turned off the engine. Mindy and I sat there in silence the only noise was the sound of the radar Ping! Ping! The contact was getting closer to us. According to the radar it was 50 feet to the west of us, but we couldn't see anything. I know the radar wasn't glitching, then suddenly we heard a loud roar.

"Oh shit! The creature is invisible to the naked eye." I said grabbing the thermal googles and tossing Mindy a pair of thermal googles.

When Mindy and I activated our thermal googles, we saw a giant 12-foot-tall beast, the hands had claws on each hand. I grabbed a gun and so did Mindy. We both got behind the vehicle and opened fired on the creature. We each shot three darts each into the creature. The creature fell when the sixth dart his it.

I walked up to the creature, pulling out a syringe and vile. I collected the creature's blood, When I touched the creature, he felt cold, but warm at the same time. This was another new species.

"Mindy, come here, check this out." I said beckoning Mindy to come see the creature closer.

Mindy reached down and touched the creature, her fac was amazed and shocked while the creature was cold and warm at the same time.

"We need to get the blood back to the lab to analyze it, but what are we going to do with this sleeping creature?" Mindy said.

"We must kill it; we can't let it live." I said getting my machete from the vehicle.

I walked back over from the vehicle with my machete in my hand. I stood over the sleeping beast. I raise my machete above my head and with a swift thrust of my arms and wrists like an executioner from the olden days that was about to chop someone's head off. I sliced into the creature's throat. Blood was spraying everywhere.

Mindy gasped at the amount of blood that was coming out of the creature's throat. I kept swinging my machete into the throat of the creature until I was sure it was fully dead.

"Let's get going to find out what else we can discover down that way." I said pointing down the long-damaged woods that we were originally heading.

Mindy stood up and went towards the vehicle, I followed shortly after. When we got to the vehicle, I started it, then suddenly Mindy got a call on her cell phone.

"Hello?" Mindy said.

"Yes, this is she." Mindy said.

I looked at her and waited until she was finished. Five minutes later, Mindy hung up the phone.

"Who was it?" I asked.

"That was another friend of ours, Gilbert. He was saying that there are reports of more Wendigos heading towards our house." Mindy said with concern in her voice.

"Shit, let's finish this and then head to the house before the Wendigos hit the house." I said.

"Okay." Mindy said.

I started the vehicle and we drove to the very end of the damage. The strange thing was that when we arrived at the end of it the damage seems to have stopped. There was undamaged dense woods in front of us. Our Geiger counters were going off. There was a reading of intense radiation indicating that a portal had opened at that exact spot.

"Looks like what we are looking for went through another portal." I said scanning the area.

"Is the portal still active?" Mindy asked.

"No, the portal is long since passed, about three hours ago to be exact." I said.

"Damn, I was hoping we could send a probe through it." Mindy said.

Chapter Eleven

While I was still taking readings, Mindy stepped off onto the side of the woods. Mindy got about six feet into the woods when she noticed a shiny steel box half buried in the ground.

"Greg, I found something over here, come help me dig it out." Mindy shouted over to me.

I put my equipment down and grabbed a shovel that we kept in our vehicle. I walked over to where I saw Mindy stand. I noticed the steel box sticking out of the ground.

"I wonder what this could be." I said starting to dig around the steel box.

After digging three feet down into the ground, we were able to remove the three-foot-long steel box from the ground. I scrapped the dirt off the lid of the box, which exposed the words "Property of the U.S. Army"

"I think we found something that give us a clue of what happen five years ago, because the box is dated from five years ago." I said.

"Let's examine it at home, it is the best place to examine it." Mindy said lifting one side of the box.

As I lifted the other side of the box, Mindy and I carried the box to the vehicle. We each got in the vehicle, and I started the vehicle. I drove down to the opening of the long-damaged woods.

When we got to the mouth of the opening, our neighbor Jamie was waiting for us there. She had a look of concern and curiosity as well on her face.

"Did you guys find anything?" Jamie asked.

"Yes, we found a new creature that was attacking us, we killed it. As well as whatever caused this damage already disappeared into another portal at the end of this damaged wood." I said.

"Okay, thank you for checking it out, I will call if more problems arise." Jamie said.

Mindy and I dare not tell Jamie about the box we found because it was classified information. Mindy and I are working together on this, we need no outsider's influences. We drove off to go to our home.

When we got home, we got out of the vehicle, Mindy and I each grabbed a side of the steel box and took it into the house. We placed it in our living room, then went back out to unload the vehicle of our equipment.

Once we have completed unloading and placing the equipment inside, I grabbed a crowbar to open the box that was a bit rushed shut. I placed the crowbar on the lock that was on the box and pulled. The lock surprisingly popped off quickly with a loud thud sound as it hit the floor. Mindy and I opened the lid, when we opened it a centipede and spiders crawled out of the box. I jumped back and smashed the spiders and centipede with the crowbar.

I turned my attention back to the steel box, there was dirt and cobwebs in the box. Mindy reached in, she pulled out a binder labeled "Red sky project". Mindy's face lit up like a kid the kid that went into a candy shop for the first time.

"We found something that will help complete our research into turning the sky back to it's normal color." Mindy said with excitement in her voice, showing me the binder, she pulled out.

I took the binder and opened it; I found a table of contents. There was a section of the binder that mentioned the side effects of the chemicals used, but there was an element that they used that was unique. It is a radioactive element designed to open portals and stabilize the red tint in the sky. It was labeled "Sethlarium", the element has Uranium, Nickel, Titanium, Mercury and some alien element that was discovered on a distant planet.

I took the binder down to the lab and scanned the information from the binder into the computer. The computer would extrapolate the reverse chemicals and elements to fix the sky.

Two minutes later a perimeter alarm was sounding, the Wendigos that our friend told us about had breached the perimeter. Our automated defense system triggered firing of rounds upon rounds of ammunition and explosives. I checked our cameras, there were over 75 Wendigo creatures converging onto our home.

Mindy grabbed our guns and we set our self-destruct system to 20 minutes. If these creatures were to over run our home along with its defenses, then the self-destruct would take them and us out in one explosion. Unfortunately, we were using a 10-kiloton nuclear bomb. It would be possible we would vaporize a big chunk of the city along with us.

Explosions and shooting went off like it was fourth of July. Roars of the Wendigos as they were hit sounded and the ceased within 18 minutes of our self-destruct timer. Mindy punched in her code to stop the self-destruct at the two-minute mark.

I checked the cameras, there were 75 dead wendigos piled on top of one another.

"Well, I better go do a cleanup, but let me do a scan to see if it is clear for us to step out." I said pulling up the radar on the computer as well as an inferred scan as we have used before.

"Looks all clear on both scans, even the aerial scan too is clear. No threats for 200 miles." I said as I got up from the desk and went up the stairs.

"Wait, keep your phone on you." Mindy said handing me my smartphone that was sitting on the desk, I had forgotten it.

"Oh yes, I forgot that, thank you my dear. I would be lost without you." I said as I turned to go up the stairs.

Chapter Twelve

When I made my way to the front door, you could already smell the burned flesh coming from under the door. I grabbed a gas mask this time. I unlocked the front door and stepped out, I could see all the bodies piled and rotting in the sunlight. The temperature was about 106 degrees outside, which made the bodies smell worse.

I put some gloves on and went around back to open the pit that we had thrown the other previous Wendigo bodies down. When I got to the back, I froze. There standing in front of me was a surviving Wendigo.

This Wendigo had burns and scratches on it's face. The Wendigo was growling at me. I slowly backed up, the Wendigo perceived that as a challenge and charged at me. I took off running, I got to my front door, I opened the door, but was met with a blow to my back with large claws. I screamed in agony, falling to the floor inside but seconds away from the Wendigo coming inside the house. I kicked the door shut.

Mindy came rushing up the basement stair, when she got to the room I was in, she saw I was on the ground bleeding.

"Hon, what happened?" Mindy said concerned getting Witch hazel, bandages, she also got the medicine that I made to heal me.

"There is a survivor Wendigo, he attacked me. I am assuming he was hiding under a pile of dead bodies when we did our scans, but that doesn't explain how he could hide from the inferred scans." I said wincing at the pain as Mindy tended to them.

After Mindy cleaned it with Witch hazel, she placed the medicine I created on them and bandaged them. I stood up, walked to the window. I saw that the Wendigo was pacing back and forth, growling at the door, then he ran at the door with a loud thud that shook the whole house.

I opened a panel on the wall by the door, punched in a code, then suddenly lasers started firing off very powerful beams. The Wendigo was sliced up like deli meat. We heard it roar and scream until it was all silent. I heard the lasers shut down on their own.

I looked at Mindy relieved, and she let out a big sigh of relieve as well.

"We are safe now." I said getting up and no longer feeling pain because I had healed from the scratches because of my medicine I created.

"This time, I am going with you outside, I'll grabbed some guns." Mindy said walking to our weapon closet.

Mindy pulled out two FN P-90 guns and two extra magazines each. Mindy walked back to me with the guns and handed me one. I walked to the door with the gun in my hand, I opened the door with the gun pointed forward, Mindy followed behind me.

When Mindy and I were outside, I pointed my gun downward and went towards the bodies to see if I could feel any air flow under the piled bodies. I reached my hand out and felt no air flow.

"We are clear with this pile of bodies, no hidden Wendigo." I said as I walked to the second pile, Mindy went to check the other two that were on the side.

There were six piles of bodies, this process took about 10 minutes to complete. We each checked and gave the all clear. I met up with Mindy by the side of the house heading towards the backyard. We of course had our guns pointing in front of us. When we got to the back it was clear of any contacts of the creatures. Mindy and I walked towards our sealed pit in the backyard.

I knelt down and unlocked the padlock and removed the chains that we used to keep the pit sealed shut. Mindy and I each grabbed a metal door and pulled them open. When opened there was a horrendous stench that escaped of charred and rotting corpses from the first kills of the first attack of Wendigos.

"We are going to need our flesh-eating acid get rid of the bodies down there." Mindy said walking back with me to start dragging bodies back.

"I agree, the incinerator is out of fuel, so the acid is the best option, about 24 gallons worth. Good thing that we have over 200 gallons of flesh-eating acid." I said walking with to the first body.

Mindy pulled out a flat bed dolly, that was we could transport the bodies to the back. I helped Mindy load one body at a time onto the dolly, while I dragged a body. We took two bodies at a time; we were outside in the hot sun for five hours moving dead bodies to the pit.

After the five hours, Mindy and I went to a shed that we had in the back with the same dolly, I unlocked the shed, Mindy and I put gloves on. We loaded the gallons, four of them at a time to the pit.

Mindy started to pour the acid down the pit, while I went to get the rest of the gallons we needed, four at a time.

The smell of the flesh being burned and dissolved by the acid was putrid and strong. Mindy and I luckily had our gas masks on. The hissing of the acids as it touched the flesh was loud, as we watched the acid dissolve the Wendigo flesh and bone. It was quite a sight, much like how the alien creature dissolves in its own acid blood in the *Alien franchise* movies.

The acid took three hours to fully dissolve the flesh of the Wendigos. Once that had completed, Mindy and I grabbed the doors to the pit and shut them. I pulled the chains over the door and padlock sealed it.

Mindy and I put away the empty gallons back into the shed, this time we could do five at a time because I could stack a fifth on top of the four that was already on the dolly. It took about twenty-five minutes to complete that task.

Chapter Thirteen

When Mindy and I finished disposing of the carcasses and the gallons of acid we used on the carcasses, we headed back towards the house.

"I am glad that we have the pit back here or we would never would have been able to dispose of those creatures." Mindy said with relieve in her voice.

"Yes, me too. Let's go get some money from of food savings jar and go get some fast food, it would be a nice treat for us, since we worked all these hours." I said.

"That would be great, I want *Wingstop* and we will stop by a *Dunkin' Donuts* for some coffee as well, I could really go for a caramel coffee from there." Mindy said.

"Sounds perfect, we should also get some *Popeyes* for me, I love the 24-piece nuggets and the 16-piece tenders as well." I said as we walked around the side of the house, heading towards the front door of the house.

When we got to the front door, Mindy stepped inside first, then me. Mindy turned to look at me.

"Before we go out to eat, we should shower." Mindy said.

"Good point, let's go shower." I said grabbing Mindy's hand leading her to the bathroom.

When we got to the bathroom, I turned Mindy towards me, I placed my hands on the bottom of her shirt and pulled up, completely removed it. I looked at her beautiful almond color skin, with beautiful size 34B breasts, perfectly shaped, I placed my hand on her breast and gently caressed them. Mindy smiled, biting her bottom lip. I moved my hands to the front of Mindy's pants and unzipped them, I pulled her pants and underwear down to her ankles, Mindy stepped out of the pants and underwear. I reached my hand to touch her beautiful almond colored vagina. I gently rubbed her vagina, Mindy let out a moan in enjoyment. Mindy grabbed my arm to stop me, and she stood me up and pulled my shirt off. She ran her hand down my chest, she could see no scars from where I used to have a shunt. The medicine I created not only removed new injuries, but old scarring as well, even it was nearly three decades old.

Mindy's hands made it's way down to my pants, She began to undo my belt, she pulled the belt out of its loops, she tossed it to the side of the bathroom. Mindy undid my pants and pulled my pants and underwear down to my ankles, she looked towards my fully erect penis, a whole 6.5-inch-long penis was staring at her. Mindy placed her hand on my penis and gently caressed it. I smiled and watched her as she was slowly caressing my penis teasing me.

Mindy looked at me in the eye as she was touching my penis. I reached my hand and began to rub her vagina. Mindy giggle, as she began to stroke my penis.

I felt the sense of pleasure that Mindy was giving me, that I almost forgot that we were supposed to shower. Mindy started to kiss my neck while she was jerking me. I reached my fingers inside of Mindy's Vagina and began to finger her, Mindy gave out a moan of pleasure.

Mindy began to jerk faster, and she was kissing down my chest, making her way to my penis. Mindy kissed my belly until she came fast to face with my penis, Mindy stared at it and began to kiss the shaft of my penis, first gently, then she would lick my shaft and she made her way to the head of my penis she gently kissed it, then opened her mouth and shoved my whole penis in her mouth. Mindy gagged and pulled away, she spit on my penis and began to jerk faster. I felt the euphoria from the pleasure I was receiving from the experience. After ten minutes of Mindy, sucking and jerking, I blew a large load of Seman all over her face, Mindy giggled as she enjoyed the feeling of the warm Seman landing on her face.

When finished Mindy got up and wiped her face into one of our shirts that were on the floor. Mindy stood up, I was still horny and still a bit dazed from the euphoria rush. I kissed Mindy on the neck and slowly made my way to her breasts. I licked and sucked her breasts, I loved the feeling of her breasts in my mouth, after a couple of minutes of me sucking her breasts, I kissed Mindy's belly.

I knelt down in front of Mindy, I had her beautiful almond colored vagina in front of my face, I began to kiss and such her vagina, Mindy giggled from the pleasure of me sucking her vagina. I moved my tongue into her vagina and made a waving a slithering motion, I felt Mindy's body shutter at the euphoria she was getting from my oral treatment. Mindy grabbed my head and shoved my head in deeper into her vagina.

I felt Mindy begin to grin on my face as she was getting close to orgasm. After ten minutes, Mindy reached orgasm and I felt her release onto my tongue. The taste was sweet and warm. The fluid was unique, I enjoyed the taste.

I stood up and saw how dazed Mindy was from the pleasurable experience, I gave her. I lead Mindy into the shower and turned on the water, we both began to wash each other.

I put *Dove* on Mindy's body as I washed her, and she put *Old Spice* on me as she washed me. We both washed every inch of each other's bodies; we took a 25-minute shower.

Chapter Fourteen

After our shower, Mindy and I got dressed, Mindy put her makeup on, then we went out to our vehicle, before we stepped out, I grabbed from our food savings jar $75 from the jar. Mindy grabbed her purse as well.

When we got in the vehicle, I started the vehicle, and we drove off. It used to be where ATV vehicles were not street legal, but laws were changed to allow all types of vehicles. I kept the speedometer at the normal road speeds, we made our way to the first restaurant stop, which was the *Wingstop*. Mindy and I stepped inside, to our surprise the restaurant was empty and not busy at all. We walked up to the counter and the cashier, who was a young black girl in her 20's started her speech.

"Hello, welcome to *Wingstop*, what would you like to order?" The young black girl said pressing keys on the register to log in.

"Yes, I would like a fifteen-piece boneless wings, that is atomic heat sauce with Louisiana heat fries. As for a drink, an extra-large Root Beer." Mindy said to the cashier.

The black girl punched in the order in the register.

"Okay, your total is $33.67." The black girl said.

I handed her two twenty-dollar bills, she gave me our receipt and my change of $6.33.

"What is the name for the order?" the cashier asked.

"Mindy." Mindy said grabbing her cup for the soda.

"Okay we will have your order out in a few minutes." The cashier said handing our order to the chief team in the kitchen in the back.

Mindy and I sat down at the closet table to the counter. I pulled Mindy's chair out for her to sit, she sat down, and I pushed the chair in. Then I went around and sat in the chair across from her.

"Well, we will need to watch a movie when we get back to relax after this long day that we have had." Mindy said.

"We will need to check our movie room to see what movie for us to watch." I said.

After twenty-five minutes, the cashier called Mindy's name for her order. The most surprising thing was that no one else walked into the restaurant, no one from *DoorDash* or any other delivery service either. I thought nothing of it, I put the thought in the back of my mind. Mindy grabbed her order and we went to the vehicle.

"Let's head over to *Popeyes* now." I said getting into the vehicle.

We pulled out of parking lot of the *Wingstop*. The *Popeyes* was only two minutes away. We arrived within two minutes, since there was hardly any traffic on the road. We pulled into the *Popeyes* parking lot. Mindy and I both stepped out of the vehicle and walked into the restaurant.

When we entered, we noticed that there was no one in the dining area of the restaurant, even at the ordering counter that was unusual, usually this restaurant, there is usually a line that is long, but it was completely empty today.

We walked up to the counter, and the Hispanic, young female cashier walked up to her register.

"Hello, what can I get you guys today?" the cashier said.

"I would like to order, a 16-piece tenders' box and 48-piece nuggets." I said.

"Any sauces? Or anything to drink?" the cashier said.

"No sauces, please and no drink, as mild seasoning on the chicken." I said.

"Okay your total is $54.86." the cashier said.

I gave the cashier the money and told her my name for the order, then Mindy and I went to a table that was closest to the second door in the restaurant. We waited about 25 minutes for the order.

25 minutes later, the cashier called my name for my order. I went up to the counter and grabbed the food, as well thanked the cashier.

We went to the vehicle and left the restaurant. On our way back home, we saw a herd of what appeared to be Griffins, these beasts had a head of an eagle, each different colors ranging from orange red to gold and white. Their wingspan was about 10 feet wide. Each Griffin had long lion like tails, about 3 feet long, each one was about 8 feet long to include tail length. These griffins were grazing off the grassy field we were passing. Mindy and I stopped the vehicle and took pictures of the majestic beasts.

"They are beautiful, let's head home before the food gets cold." I said almost forgetting we had food in the vehicle.

"Okay, I'm starving." Mindy said as we drove off.

Chapter Fifteen

When Mindy and I pulled up to our home, I parked the vehicle in the front of the house. Shut the car off and grabbed the food. Mindy got ahead of me to unlock the house.

We walked inside, then went towards the kitchen to get some plates for our food. We of course washed plates and utensils before using them, because of our past experience we each had with an invasive species of cockroaches crawling all over our plates and utensils.

Even though we have a completely pest free home, the habit has stuck with us. We washed up two plates and two forks. I dried them and set them out. Mindy filled her plate with her food and so did I.

"What do you want to watch?" I said grabbing the plates.

"Well, let's go check our movie library." Mindy said as she carried her soda and my water to the movie library.

We went down a small hallway and then came to a door, a normal white door. Mindy opened it and there were shelves lining the walls of the 15x18 foot room. There were a few shelves in the middle of the room and a pedestal with a large book in the middle of the room. Mindy walked up to it and started going through the book that had the title of every movie and series that we own. Approximately 1000 or so titles were in that book.

"Ah, let's watch *Night of the Living Dead (1990)*, then we should watch *Stargate(1994), Tremors(1990).*"Mindy said going over to the shelves the movies were at and collecting them.

Mindy and I went to our home theater that we had custom build, which has gotten 1000 times cheaper since the sky has turned red. Especially since the population has dropped considerably, and there was less demand for stuff, and labor was cheaper too.

We had a 120-inch theater screen on the wall, with the best speakers, the walls were designed like the *Stargate Atlantis* gate room, with air popper for popcorn, we had a minifridge next to the air popper for drinks, as well as a shelf full of other snacks. We had a bed placed in the theater instead of theater seats, because it is more comfortable to watch movies laying down on the bed than in a stiff seat.

Mindy laid down on the bed with the food as I went to put in the movie *Night of the living dead (1990)*. After I put the movie in, I went to the bed to lay down and began to eat my food. The movie started with the main characters visiting their deceased mother's grave. As we watch we both began to eat our foods.

Meanwhile, down in the basement lab, the computer had finished compiling the data from the data it analyzed to figure out the reversal on the sky's color. An alarm went off to alert us that it was finished.

Mindy and I heard the alarm right when the movie was getting to the good part.

"Darn it, it was getting good, good thing we finished our food." I said pausing the movie and getting off the bed.

Mindy looked at me with a sleepy look on her face from eating the food.

"You take a nap; I will go check out what the alarm is about." I said kissing her on the head and laying her back down and tucked her in.

I stepped out of the theater and went down the hall to the kitchen, I went to the door that led to the basement lab. I opened the door and went down the stairs.

When I got to the bottom of the stairs, I went to the desk where the computer was still blaring with the alarm. I shut off the alarm and the screen started to display technical ingredients for the reversal of the sky.

I printed off the list of the reversal proceedings. There were about 12 pages of instructions, to include ingredients we would need to reverse the sky color. It appeared that we would need high grade Rathium, it is a radioactive element that reverses the effects of Sethlarium, that was used originally. Both elements are radioactive of course, except the Rathium is a polar opposite of Sethlarium.

The other ingredients we would need is a powerful rocket, and some acids which are not hard to obtain. I grinned and quickly took the papers upstairs with me to inform Mindy. I rushed up the stairs, I rushed to the theater excited to tell Mindy the news.

I turned into the theater and jumped on the bed like a child that was excited for Christmas morning.

"Mindy, wake up, honey. The computer finished it's extrapolation. We have a way to reverse the sky." I said gently nudging Mindy to awaken.

When I said that Mindy darted up like a bullet. The look on her face was shock, mixed with a bit if excitement.

"We have the cure for the sky? I am excited. Let me see the papers." Mindy said taking the papers from my hands.

As Mindy examined them, her face grew more excited like we had found the lost city of Atlantis.

"Sweet, I know where we can get our hands on both the elements we need." Mindy said.

"Okay, where can we get it? I will get the computer to start building the rocket, and we already have the acids and the other ingredients that are needed." I said.

"We must visit the other military base that is on the east side of town, when the car is ready. We should have all this built in two weeks." Mindy said getting off the bed.

"Good, why can't we use the vehicle we have to go to the base?" I asked.

"The vehicle isn't fast enough in case we encounter more Wendigos." Mindy said.

Chapter Sixteen

Two days later, the car was ready for us, the mechanic dropped the car off at our house for us around 8 a.m. Mindy and I paid the mechanic before he was driven back in another vehicle.

Once the mechanic left, Mindy and I started to load the car up for the trip to the abandoned military base. Mindy and I grabbed our P-90 weapons, grenades, knives and water as well as food for the trip.

We got in the car and drove off. While we were driving Mindy was watching the onboard radar that we had in the car. The radar was clear for about 20 miles.

"Do you have the map for the base?" I asked while driving the car.

"Yes, I have it marked on where the lab is at." Mindy said keeping her eyes on the radar.

We drove 30 minutes to the abandon base that we were heading towards. When we arrived at the abandon base, I parked the car and got out of the car, walked up to the closed gate. I saw a lock and chain on the gate. I turned back to the car, opened the trunk of the car and pulled out bolt cutters. I walked back to the gate and snapped the rusted lock, and the chain fell down to the ground. I opened the gate and then went back to the car and drove through the gate.

Mindy opened her map of the base; she scanned it for a moment and then told me we should head to the west side of the base and in the middle of the west side is where the lab is located. I drove on towards the west side of the base, which took about ten minutes to get to there.

When we arrived at a large building, the building was a bland brown color, Mindy and I parked the car in the front of the abandoned building. I turned off the car, we stepped out of the car and started gathering flashlights, P-90's, and bolt cutter. We walked up to the brown metal doors that were in the front of the building, that were, of course sealed with a lock and chain, just like the front gates.

I cut the rusted lock off the chain and as before the chain fell to the ground and opened the door. The metal door creaked from not being in use for five years, let alone being taken care of.

Mindy shined her flashlight into the dark room, I shined mine as well. Mindy entered in first with her P-90 pointing forward. We are cautious because we don't know what to expect in places that have been abandoned.

Same as the last abandoned base, the building had a small entry lobby. There was a small window for you to sign in at like the other base. Mindy and I walked down about six feet until we came to where there was a turn that lead to double doors, behind those doors was where the labs were at. These double doors required for you to have a key card to open the doors, since they were heavy metal doors as well.

"We have no power in the building, let alone a key card. Go back to the car and get the C4 explosive, about three of them." Mindy said.

I turned to step out of the building to go back to the car. When I stepped outside my eyes were met with sunlight, it was the normal reaction to the light since I was in a dark building. I quickly went to the car, I went to the trunk, opened the trunk. I grabbed four of the C4 explosive in case we would need it, but before I closed the trunk, I pause for the moment, and it dawned on me to take the whole case of 36 C4 explosives with me.

When I got back inside, Mindy was still standing at the double doors. I set the case down and opened it. I pulled out three of the C4 explosive out. I placed them on the door.

"Okay, lets get over there." I pointed as I armed the explosives.

Mindy and I went behind the wall to a safe distance. I pulled out the trigger remote and flipped the switch. A loud explosion came roaring forward with flames that reached about three feet from the door, the building shook a little from the vibrations.

When the flames cleared, Mindy and I looked around the corner, where the double doors were. The doors were destroyed with a large hole made in the middle of them, large enough for us to walk through.

"Okay, moving forward. By the way, why did you bring the full case of C4?" Mindy asked walking through the hole in the doors.

"I have a feeling we might need the whole case with us, you don't know if there are other doors like this one." I said stepping through the hole in the doors.

Mindy and I preceded down a long dark hallway, there was an eerie feeling as we went deeper and deeper into the dark hallway, I had a very dark feeling like something, as if wasn't right down this hallway. I stepped for a moment; I felt a tightness on my chest as if something was squeaking it. Mindy stopped and turned to me, with a concerned look on her face.

"What is wrong?" Mindy said placing her hand on my shoulder.

"I have a bad feeling and a tightness in my chest." I said trying to breath.

"It must mean we are close to where we need to go." Mindy said shining her flashlight down the long hallway.

I was fighting to get the tightness to stop, I couldn't let this stop us from our mission. I tried to move, but it was getting to be unbearable.

"Look, stay here, I can't have you go any further, I will stay in walkie talkie communication with you. You get back to the lobby, I will go further ahead." Mindy said turning on her walkie talkie.

"Okay, are you sure?" I said turning my walkie talkie.

"Yes, I am sure. I can't have you die here. I need you safe." Mindy said walking down the hallway.

As Mindy was walking down the hallway, I turned to head back to the lobby door. As I got closer to the door, the tightness in my chest got lighter. By the time, I was at the door the tightness disappeared. I radioed Mindy.

"Honey, the tightness is gone." I said over the radio.

"Something was warning you; I believe, I will find what we need in this first lab, that I am about to enter." Mindy radioed back to me.

As I waited for Mindy at the entrance of the hallway, I heard something moving down the hallway in the direction of Mindy.

"Honey, be careful, I just heard something moving down in your direction." I said over the walkie talkie.

"I am good, I didn't hear anything, I am just opening a safe, that has quite a bit of combination on it. I think the elements are in there, the Geiger counter is going off." Mindy said.

Worry started to take over, I took a deep breath, gathered the strength to handle the pain from whatever it is that was hurting me. I ran down the hallway and began to feel the tightness on my chest again. I tried to fight the squeezing on my chest. The closer I got to the lab Mindy was in the tightness got tighter, until I entered the lab and the tightness stopped, which stop abruptly. I was standing in the doorway of the lab, looking back in the hallway, confused.

Mindy turned around from the safe and looked at me, with a surprised look on her face.

"I thought you couldn't cross hallway. What changed?" Mindy said with confusion in her voice.

"That is the thing, I felt a squeezing on my chest all the way down here, until I got in this room. I have a theory that it has to do with those elements. Whatever was squeezing me is repelled by the elements." I said.

"That is strange. Come help me open this safe, please." Mindy said.

I walked over to the safe and saw that the safe was not only a regular combination lock, but there is a runic code as well, even an Egyptian Hieroglyphic code too. I immediately reconsidered.

Chapter Seventeen

"I know how to unlock this safe." I said moving the Egyptian Hieroglyphics, then the runic symbols into place.

Once I placed both sets of symbols into place, the safe began to open on it's own with a whining sound. Mindy's eyes got huge at the surprise that I could unlock the safe.

"How did you know how to unlock the safe?" Mindy asked with curiosity in her voice.

"Well, I have studied both Egyptian Hieroglyphics and runic symbols." I said.

Once the safe was completely open, it exposed a series of 24 glass vials each of both elements on the three-shelf safe. Mindy opened a duffle bag; we began to load the duffle bag with the vials of the elements that we needed. As we emptied the safe, I noticed a small metal box that was sealed, I didn't know what was inside of it, but I did pack it into the duffle bag.

We zipped up the duffle bag and started our way out of the lab. When we got out in the hallway, I was shocked to not feel the tightness on my chest. Mindy looked at me. She was surprised that I didn't say I felt the tightness on my chest.

"My theory was right, whatever it was making my chest tight, is afraid of the elements we now have in the duffle bag." I said as we walked down the hall.

As we went through the hole in the double doors, we heard a loud roar behind us. I looked back and saw standing at the end of the hall was a Wendigo.

"GO TO THE CAR!!!" I shouted as I was shooting and running from the Wendigo.

The Wendigo began pursuing us as we ran to the car, I through a C4 explosive that landed on the Wendigo and flipped the switch and blew the Wendigo beast away, guts and body parts went everywhere. Mindy and I made our way back to the car. I secured the duffle bag of the elements that we needed in the back seat of the car.

As I got in the driver seat of the car, another Wendigo stepped out of the building, it looked left then right at us. It growled. I grabbed a grenade and threw it at the Wendigo. The Wendigo caught the grenade in it's mouth, then the grenade exploded killing the Wendigo, by blowing it's head clean off.

I started the car and drove off before any other Wendigos could come out of the building.

"We succeeded our mission; the sky is going to go back to normal." Mindy said.

"Yes, I am happy, we have won." I said, suddenly I coughed, and blood was in my hand.

I wiped the blood on my pants, I was hoping Mindy didn't noticed. Of course, she didn't notice the blood she was busy looming out the window.

As we kept driving, we remained quiet until we got home. I got out of the car, went to the back seat and pulled out the duffle bag. Mindy went to the front door and unlocked the door. We both walked in and walked down to the basement lab. When we got down in the basement lab, I put the duffle bag on a table that was empty in the lab. I unzipped the bag and began to unpack the bag. I placed alle the vials of elements out on the table.

"How soon can we get the rocket we will need built?" I asked.

"Well, I got the nanobots to build the rocket while we were out, it is ready to be loaded. The nanobots work fast." Mindy said getting the rocket out of the glass case it was in, which is where the nanobots did their work.

I pulled the small metal box out of the duffle bag as well. I saw a small lock that is usually used for luggage. I quickly snapped the lock off and opened the box. Inside the box was a vial of a strange red liquid, the liquid also had a metallic hue to it. I grabbed a Perti dish and Q-tip. I placed a slide into the Petri dish, I then took the Q-tip, opened the vial and got a small drop of the liquid, them smeared it onto the slide. I took the slide to an analyzer that we had in the lab.

"What is that liquid?" Mindy said.

"I don't know, I am scanning it to see if we get an answer, shouldn't be that long to analyze it." I said getting a glass container and began placing the ingredients into it for the rocket.

After ten minutes, the analyzer dinged and began to print off what it had discovered. I grabbed the print off and found out what was causing the creatures we have been seeing to come into our world was this liquid. The liquid is not of this dimensional plane. The analyzed predicts that if we put the liquid in the rocket, it would close the portals and no more creatures coming into our world.

"Honey, we have found the cause of the portals, it is this liquid, it isn't from our dimension. The analyze predicts that if we put it in the rocket, the portals will be shut." I said.

"Good, we will use the whole vial of it. I think that will work." Mindy said.

I started loading the elements and other ingredients including the vial of strange liquid into the glass container. Once I filled the container, I sealed it, and placed an explosive on the glass to be detonated once pressure triggers it from the atmosphere. I placed the container into the rocket. We sealed the rocket and took it outside.

Mindy and I walked to a clearing in our yard, we set the rocket up for launch. Once the rocket was ready for launch, I punched the count down timer on the side of the rocket and on a laptop that we brought with us. Mindy and I stood back about three yards away from the rocket.

As the rocket hit the last seconds of the countdown, flames were shooting out of the bottom of the rocket and lifting it off the ground. We watched the rocket, and it was getting higher and higher in the air. Within ten minutes, the rocket reached its destination, and detonated in the air. There were colors of red, green, orange and blue.

I hugged Mindy and gave her a large kiss for the successful launch. We knew that the sky would need time to repair itself and the sky wouldn't go back to normal right away.

Mindy and I turned and walked back towards the house; Mindy was ahead of me about a foot ahead of me when my nose began to bleed. I pulled out a handkerchief and quickly whipped my nose. Before I could hide the blood-soaked handkerchief, Mindy turned around and saw it and began to panic.

"What happened? Where did that blood come from?" Mindy said running up to me to see if I am okay, but before I could answer her my nose was bleeding more and my ears.

Mindy grabbed my arm and pulled me as hard as she could to where we were running towards the house.

"I need to get you the medicine we have made to heal you, quickly." Mindy said panicking tugging harder.

When we got to the house, Mindy kicked the door in and dragged me through the door, she sat me on a chair with my nose and ears still bleeding, she handed me a towel while she went to get the medication that would heal me. When she got back to me, blood was coming out of my fingernails.

I quickly took the medication; I was close to passing out from all the blood loss. Within 20 minutes, after taking the medication the bleeding stopped.

"When did you first notice the bleeding?" Mindy asked me.

"The first time was when we were driving back from the base." I said.

"Why didn't you tell me?" Mindy asked.

"I didn't think it would get this bad. I thought it was a minor thing, I think it was a radiation thing from being exposed to the liquid in the vial, now that I think about it." I said.

Mindy stared at me a shook her head in agreement.

"I believe so too, but your body is more sensitive to things like that, unlike mine." Mindy said.

Chapter Eighteen

Mindy and I began to cook dinner, the time was about 4:30pm, when we began cooking. I pulled out two Cornish game hens, seasoned them up with garlic powder, and garlic salt. I place them in the oven at 500 degrees for 30 minutes.

Mindy went out to our garden to harvest so onions, bell peppers, and cilantro. While she was outside harvesting, she started to notice that the sky was changing from red to green to orange, then finally back to blue. A big grin came across Mindy's face. She darted into to house with the onions she had collected in her hand.

"Greg come outside, IT WORKED!" Mindy said excitedly.

I turned around and followed Mindy outside and saw that the sky had indeed turned back to blue. Mindy and I hugged each other in excitement. We turned to go back inside and turned the television news on with headlines "SKY TURNS BACK TO BLUE" on every news channel, there was footage of people rejoicing at the sky returning back to blue.

After that initial day of the sky turning back to blue, the government officials kept saying it was not permanent, the sky would turn back to red, but Mindy and I's instruments said it was permanently fixed. The government was spinning lies and trying to bring everyone down.

In the coming months, the other countries were returning back to the earth to reclaim their original land. A large world war had broken out, when each country discovered the United States of America had stolen their land.

The war lasted twenty five years, until the United States of America had come to an agreement to return the taken land back to the countries, but as long as they could have mineral rights to all minerals in those lands.

Mindy and I were happy that we didn't have to get chased by beasts from other dimensions anymore. Speaking of the beasts that were trapped here on this side of the dimension. Our government created a Cryptoid Zoo for all to see of these unique creatures. Classic Mankind always caging and displaying creatures for entertainment.

Mindy and I opened our own business of paranormal investigations, and we rake in thousands of dollars everyday and get hundreds of calls across the world.

So, we travel a lot investigating the paranormal, we have published hundreds of books on our research we had done during the time the sky was red. In fact, the government still wants everyone to believe that they are right that the sky will turn red again. It has already been six years since Mindy, and I have fixed the sky.

THE END.

www.ingramcontent.com/pod-product-compliance
Lightning Source LLC
Chambersburg PA
CBHW012024110726
47994CB00012B/3299